Introduction

Iris the Dragon (**Charity**) was created to provide educational material for adults and young readers to help facilitate a conversation between parents, teachers and children about issues relating to mental health and wellness. Iris the Dragon's books address a variety of emotional, behavioural and neurodevelopmental conditions and recognize the importance of family, school, and community in promoting the potential of every child and youth, regardless of mental health challenge. Support of children's mental health initiatives promotes positive youth development, recovery, and resilience, and allows children with mental health needs to thrive in their communities.

Our latest book "I Can Fix It a tale from the Iris the Dragon Series" focuses on educating our audiences about Asperger's Syndrome, one of the **Autism Spectrum Disorders** (**ASD**). Once again, Iris helps the central character in the book a little girl called Josie who has Asperger's Syndrome. But Iris also tackles the challenge of getting the whole community to support and understand what children with various mental health conditions are confronted with in life with the introduction of **The Brave New Minds Walk**. The book has been vetted by the Dual Diagnostic Team at CHEO (Children's Hospital of Eastern Ontario) and an informative epilogue about ASD has been provided by Dr. Mark Kaluzienski. In addition, the book is endorsed by Dr. Peter Szatmari and Dr. Simon Davidson.

We recommend that the parent, teacher or caregiver read the epilogue on pages 45-48 before reading this book with the child. The information provided by Dr. Kaluzienski will help the reader to answer questions that the child may have about the topic.

Iris the Dragon Book Series

Catch a Falling Star a tale from the Iris the Dragon Series - 2000

Lucky Horseshoes a tale from the Iris the Dragon Series - 2007

Hole in One a tale from the Iris the Dragon Series - 2008

I Can Fix It a tale from the Iris the Dragon Series – 2009

Contact Information:

info@iristhedragon.com www.iristhedragon.com

Acknowledgements

Iris the Dragon is very grateful to the many people and agencies who supported the writing of this book. As with all Iris the Dragon books, it is very important that the facts on children's mental health disorders are presented accurately and with compassion. The following people were instrumental in ensuring the above.

Dr. Ian Manion, Executive Director, the Provincial Centre of Excellence for Child and Youth Mental Health at CHEO (Children's Hospital of Eastern Ontario).

Dr. Simon Davidson, M.B., B.Ch., F.R.C.P.(C), Professor of Psychiatry and Paediatrics, Chairman, Division of Child and Adolescent Psychiatry, University of Ottawa; Chief Strategic Planning Executive, Provincial Centre of Excellence for Child and Youth Mental Health at the Children's Hospital of Eastern Ontario.

Dr. Peter Szatmari Professor and Head, Division of Child Psychiatry in the Department of Psychiatry and Behavioural Neurosciences at McMaster University, where he holds the Chedoke Health Chair in Child Psychiatry. He is Director of the Offord Centre of Child Studies.

Dual Diagnosis TEAM at CHEO - Ms. Jennifer Boggett OT reg. (ONT), Occupational Therapist, Dual Diagnosis Team; Dr. Michael Cheng, MD, FRCP (C), Assistant Professor, Department of Psychiatry, University of Ottawa Child Psychiatrist, Mood and Anxiety Team, Children's Hospital of Eastern Ontario; Dr. Yasser Ad-Dab'bagh, MD, (FRCP (C), Assistant Professor, Department of Psychiatry, University of Ottawa, Child Psychiatrist, Dual Diagnosis Team, Children's Hospital of Eastern Ontario; Dr. Margaret Flintoff, Ph.D. Psychologist, Dual Diagnosis Team; Dr. Mark Kaluzienski, M.D., FRCP(C), Psychiatrist, Fellow Dual Diagnosis Clinic, Children's Hospital of Eastern Ontario; Ms. Nicole Roberts, Reg CASLPO, SLP – (C), Speech-Language Pathologist, Dual Diagnosis Team; Ms. Charlotte Savage, Registered Nurse (RN), Dual Diagnosis Team;

Nicki Collins, Executive Director, Open Doors for Lanark Children and Youth; Ms. Kelsey Doyle, Instructor Therapist, Surrey Place Centre; Ms. Margaret Howard, Director, TPAS, Surrey Place Centre;

Ms Miriam Silvert and students from Room 15, Yorkview Public School, Dundas, Ontario, Board Member of OASAR – The Ontario Association for Children at Risk

a tale from the Iris the Dragon Series

A Children's Book Dealing with Asperger's Syndrome and Stigma

written by **Gayle Grass** illustrated by **Graham Ross**

And the Introduction of the Iris Cards Anti-Stigma Campaign for all children with Mental Health Challenges

SPRING

Once upon a time there lived a very special, magical, green, marsh dragon called Iris. She was very old and wise, and lived in the Riverbank Community, in a cave, under an old log bridge. The Riverbank was a peaceful community where the animals had learned that to live together, they should be polite, trustworthy and caring of one another.

Today was a special day for Iris as it was her 909th birthday, and all the Riverbank animals had come to celebrate. Even some special human friends were there, Teeman, Fish and Skippy. Iris had helped them overcome their mental health challenges to achieve their dreams. They were all sitting on their favourite log outside Iris's cave chatting and laughing when all of a sudden they heard loud angry voices on the bridge.

"You are so stupid. You can't play with us. You act and talk funny and you are a big crybaby," yelled a boy.

"And we don't like you either," said another mean voice. **"Here, go fetch your bike."**

Suddenly, Iris and her friends heard a loud splash in the water under the bridge, followed by another splash.

Iris flew to the edge of the bank and dove in the water. She was followed by Ottie Otter and Madeleine Frog who were all very good swimmers. Iris swam under the bridge and saw a little girl splashing around in the water. She was very upset and scared.

“Here, take hold of my wing and climb on my back,” said Iris.

“They’re so mean! They threw my Mongoose™ BMX Bike in the water. My very special bike, so I had to jump in after it!” screamed the little girl.

Iris gently secured the little girl between her wings and swam toward the shore. As they neared it, Teeman, Fish and Skippy were there to help the little girl onto the riverbank.

“Please take her to the log and I will get some blankets from my cave,” said Iris.

When Iris returned, she noticed that the little girl was still very upset and was stomping back and forth along the riverbank muttering to herself and shaking her fist at the boys as they tore down the road. “I hate those boys and their stupid tricks,” yelled the little girl still shaking with rage.

“Is she alright Iris?” asked Ottie Otter. “She is really upset.”

“I think our new guest has a condition that when she gets upset, she sometimes gets very angry. Let’s give her some space and time to calm down,” said Iris.

After a while, the little girl stopped pacing and muttering to herself and looked over at the Riverbank Animals and Iris. "Hi," said Iris. "You are safe here. No one will hurt you. My name is Iris and this is Teeman, Fish and Skippy and here are the Riverbank animals as well. What is your name?"

"Josie," said the little girl in an angry voice.

"That is a pretty name. Would you like to talk to us?" asked Iris.

Josie remained silent for a few minutes. She was still very frightened and agitated. Then she blurted out, "they are so mean. They threw my bike in the river! Look at it. It is all messed up."

"Well Josie, come and put on this warm blanket and we can talk about it," answered Iris.

Josie came over to the log and accepted the blanket from Iris and wrapped it tightly around herself. After a few minutes, she looked up, and for the first time really noticed Iris.

"Iris, you look like a big green dragon," said Josie. "I have a book about dragons. My dragon book says that there are three general classes of dragons. There are the European Dragons, the Asiatic Dragons and the Tropical Dragons. They can fly and breathe fire. Can you?" asked Josie.

"I am from the class of European Dragons and the family of Green Marsh Dragons. I can fly and breathe fire also," replied Iris.

"Wow, that is so cool," exclaimed Josie.

"Would you like to meet some of my Riverbank friends?" Iris asked, hoping that this would help Josie relax and feel safe. "This is Ottie Otter. He never stops talking, but likes to make sure everyone is OK in the Riverbank. This little creature is Madeleine Frog. She likes to bake and share her goodies with everyone. Over there, behind the log, is Rosie Raccoon. She is very shy. Beside Ottie is Freddy Fox and here beside me is Becky Rabbit and Chippy Chipmunk. We are all friends and if anyone needs help we are there for each other."

"You are lucky that you have friends," said Josie. "I don't think people like me very much. They say I act funny and sometimes they play tricks on me because they know that they can fool me."

"What do they say to you Josie?" questioned Iris.

"Well, they say I am no fun to play with because I have to follow the rules. I don't like it when kids try to play a game and change the rules. It makes me mad," explained Josie.

"People can say mean things," said Iris. "We had a little trouble here a few years ago. We had some new animals move into our Riverbank Community and at first it seemed like they were very inconsiderate."

"I remember them," exclaimed Ottie.
"Tell Josie who they were."

"Well, they were the River Rat Brothers. When they arrived, they were very noisy and kept their neighbours up all night. In fact, it was so bad that Becky Rabbit and her family had to move to another borough. We had a meeting and decided to show them that animals don't have to act like that to be noticed," said Iris.

"I don't like loud noises either. I can't stand it when my parents vacuum and I hate the school bus when it gets really noisy," interrupted Josie.

Iris smiled at Josie and continued. "So we sent them an invitation to a tea party. Some of the Riverbank animals thought I should use my magic and make them disappear, but I said: using force never solves anything. We have to educate them to understand that we can all live in the same community even though we are all different in some ways."

"Did they come to the tea party, Iris?" asked Josie. "I would like to come to your tea party. What did you have to eat?"

"Yes, they did Josie. We prepared a wonderful feast of slimy green marsh sandwiches, dandelion milkshakes and bulrush insect pie. Those noisy River Rats were shocked that we wanted them to come to our party. No one had been nice to them in quite a long time," explained Iris. "And guess what? It turns out they thought they were being nice by sharing their music with everyone else! So when they found out that other people didn't like the same loud music that they did, they turned their music down. And then things got better after that. So you see Josie, there is sometimes a reason why people act mean. Sometimes, it's because they've been treated badly. But many other times, it's because they just don't know any better."

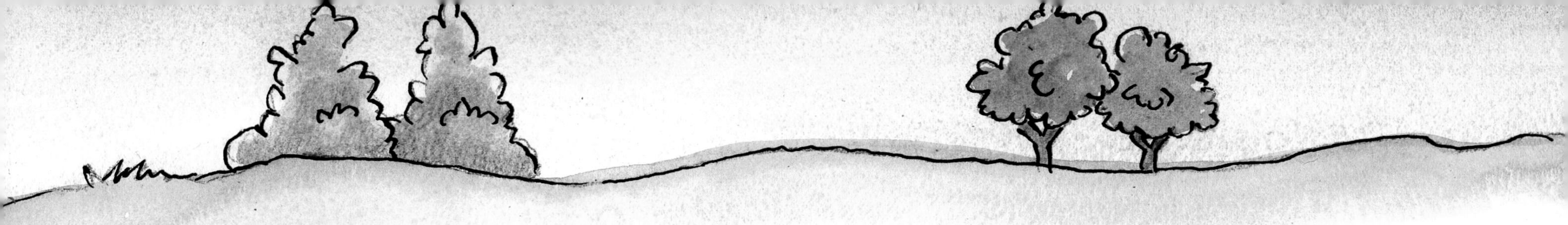

"Well, my parents are always saying that people are mean to me because I have Asperger's Syndrome. Do you know what that is?" said Josie.

"As a matter of fact Josie, I do. I have a book about Autism Spectrum Disorders (ASDs) and Asperger's Syndrome is one of the disorders on the spectrum. I know that children with Asperger's Syndrome sometimes say things that don't make sense to other people and then those people get upset with you. But there are tools to help you be understood and we can educate people about Asperger's Syndrome so they understand why you act the way you do. Now, you had better get home before you catch a cold," said Iris as she looked over at Josie's bike. "Oh dear, your bike is broken. You can leave it here and I will try and fix it for you."

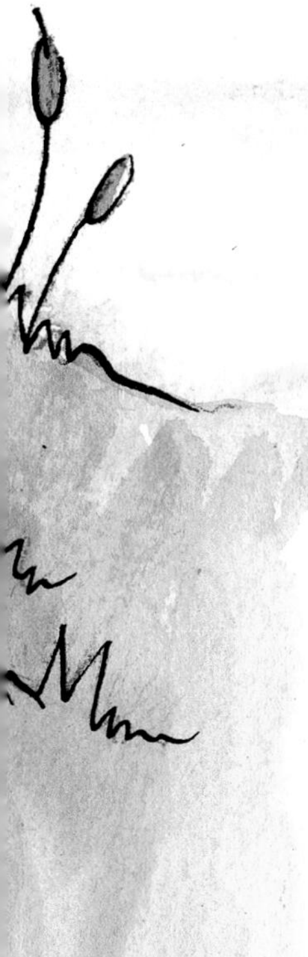

"I can fix it Iris. I will come back tomorrow with my tools," said Josie. **"I can fix anything."**

"Well that is wonderful as I have a shed full of things that need fixing. I will arrange for one of the children to come and get you so your parents don't worry," said Iris.

"That would be great, Iris, as I really like to fix things. Bye Iris and all the Riverbank Animals. See you tomorrow," said Josie.

"We'll walk Josie home, Iris!" said Teeman.

After the children left, Ottie Otter said to Iris,

**“What are we going to do, Iris?
Those boys were so mean to her!”**

“I know Ottie, but I have an idea. Let’s have a Riverbank meeting tomorrow to discuss it. Thank you, so much, for my birthday party. I had a wonderful time. Good night, my friends,” waved Iris as she scurried to her cave. She wanted to get started on her plan right away.

Iris stayed up all night looking through her books of knowledge for answers. She knew she could help Josie practice how to be with other people and learn social skills, but how do you teach the town to treat children with mental health challenges with respect and include them in the activities of the community? Finally she thought of a plan. When the Riverbank animals arrived, she told them to take a seat and handed each of them a little case with a picture of an Iris flower on the cover.

“What is this Iris?” asked Madeleine Frog.

“I am hoping these cases will help Josie and other children with mental health challenges. We need to educate people about the various children’s mental health disorders. For example, Josie has an Autism Spectrum Disorder which is a neurodevelopmental condition – it is not her fault that she has it,” explained Iris. “For example, when Josie thinks she is just trying to be nice, other people see her as being rude. Because Josie loves bikes so much, she thinks that everyone else must like bikes, too. So she tries to tell everyone she knows all about bikes and how they work, because she thinks that will make people like her. But then the children get bored, and she doesn’t realize that she should stop talking. Worse, when people roll their eyes and say sarcastic things like. “Josie. That is SO INTERESTING,” she doesn’t understand that they’re really trying to say the opposite – to STOP TALKING about bikes. So the question is: How do we help people understand children with mental health challenges?

My plan is in these little cases.

You can open them now,” said Iris.

Madeleine opened her case and took out a card. On one side was a picture of an Iris flower and on the other there was writing.

You are being given this card because we have noticed that you have done a very kind deed today. You have been kind to a child that has a mental health challenge and needed your help and assistance. You have taken the first step in educating yourself about these special children.

Thank you.

If you see someone who also does a kind deed for a child would you pass this card onto them?

Your friend
Iris

"Should I read it, Iris?"

"Yes, please, Madeleine," smiled Iris.

"It says," read Madeleine. "You are being given this card because we have noticed that you have done a very kind deed today. You have been kind to a child that has a mental health challenge and needed your help and assistance. You have taken the first step in educating yourself about these special children. Thank you. If you see someone who also does a kind deed for a child would you pass this card onto them?

Signed, Your friend, Iris."

"Iris, who do we give these to?" asked Freddy Fox.

"We are to carry them with us all the time and if we see someone in the village doing a good deed for one of these children, we are to slip one in their pocket," said Iris. "I am hoping that this will raise awareness about children with mental health challenges."

"That is a great idea, Iris.
This will be fun.
When can we start?"

asked Tommie Turtle who had just arrived at the meeting. "I have to get started soon if I want to reach the town before nightfall."

"Right away!

Take your cards and see how many you can give out today. We will keep a record of all the people that receive the cards and see if the town becomes more aware and understanding of these children," said Iris.

"We have a lot of work to do.
So let's gets started."

Iris handed out the cases of cards to all the Riverbank animals. They had all come to help. There was Mr. Coyote, the River Rat Brothers, Rosie Raccoon, Freddy Fox, Madeleine Frog, Becky Rabbit, Petunia Skunk, Dora Duck, Bobbie Beaver, Mr. Toad, Georgie Groundhog, Ottie Otter and all the other animals in the Riverbank Community. They were all excited about this project and were all going to work together to make it successful. So they took off to observe people in the town to see if they could find someone to give a card to.

Ottie Otter was the first to see a good deed. Hidden under the bridge in the middle of the town, he saw Skippy, who he knew had ADHD, looking very confused, standing on her front porch. Just then Skippy's neighbour came up to her and asked if she needed help. Skippy said she had left her knapsack at the stables where she took care of Little Ben and her front door key was in it. Her mom wouldn't be home for a while. The neighbour offered to drive her back to the stables to get her key and as they got into the car, Ottie ran up and quickly put an Iris Card in the woman's pocket.

Throughout the day, the Riverbank animals put the Iris Cards in the villager's pockets. Madeleine was especially ecstatic when she saw a teenager defending a child with a mental health disorder being bullied in the school yard. She jumped up and put an Iris Card in his pocket and quickly hopped away before he noticed her. Iris was very proud of her team and told them they were off to a good start.

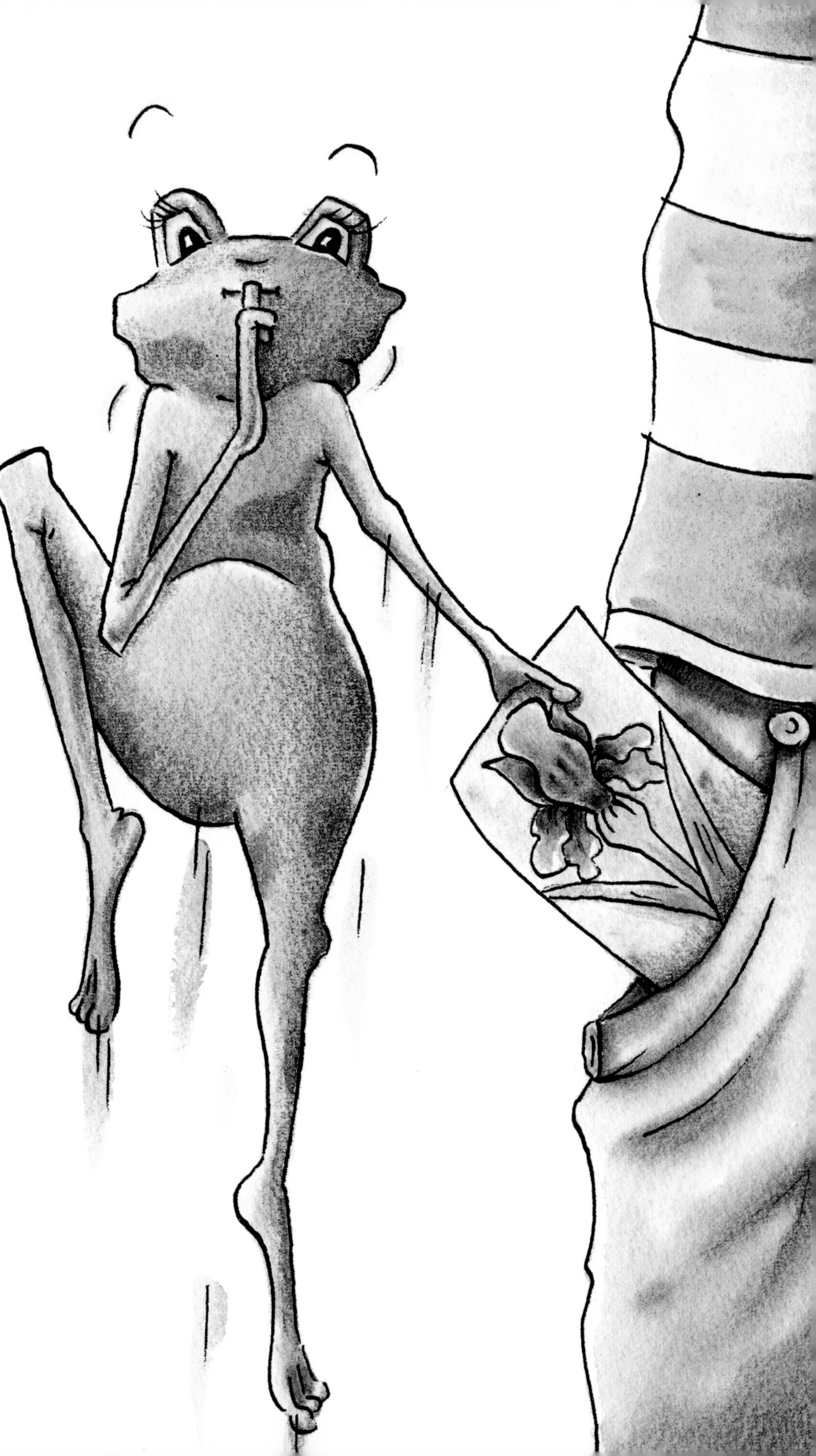

The next day, Teeman escorted Josie to the Riverbank so she could fix her bike.

"I'll be back in an hour to take you home," said Teeman. "I promised your mom that I would not let you get lost."

"Don't worry, Teeman," said Josie. "I wear this special bracelet that tells people that I have Asperger's and how to contact my parents. My mom says it is very important that I wear it all the time."

"That sounds like a good idea. I will still be back in an hour Josie. See ya!" said Teeman.

"Hi Josie," said Iris as she appeared at her cave door. "Just take a seat on the log. I will get your bike and my broken lawn mower for you to fix."

Josie sat on the log and noticed how peaceful it was. The birds were singing and the river was flowing gently by. She liked being by herself as she did not get overwhelmed when she was alone. When there were a lot of people around, her brain seemed to stop working and this got her upset. But she did not feel like this with Iris. Iris was very peaceful to be with.

“OK, here they are,” said Iris.

“I like to fix things Iris. I am very good at taking things apart and putting them together again so they work. I have taken my bike apart many times. My bike is a Mongoose™ BMX bike and has full suspension of 90 mm. Did you know that the first suspension forks weren’t introduced until the 1990’s? Both my front and rear suspension works by pneumatic shocks. I will need to take them apart and clean them. I will show you what I mean,” said Josie as she told Iris all about her bike for the next several minutes.

Finally Iris said, “you know so much about bikes, Josie. I’m going to guess you’ve really worked hard at learning about bikes.”

“I try to tell my classmates about all these things and they get mad at me. My classmates even call me Josie Stupid! But I am not stupid. I know a lot more about bikes then they do. But I wish I could figure out people like I can figure out bikes,” said Josie.

“I agree Josie, you are definitely not stupid and in fact, you have a lot of special strengths. What if I could teach you how to figure out people and you help me fix all my broken equipment?” asked Iris. “I can teach you some tips on how to make friends and keep from getting teased.”

“I like that idea, Iris,” agreed Josie.

Throughout the summer, Josie would often come to the Riverbank and help Iris fix her many contraptions that she had collected over the years. She even had one of the very first computers that was ever made, an old Apple IIe,™ and Josie loved to take it apart and put it together again.

While Josie worked on the machines, Iris taught Josie social skills. Iris knew that Asperger's was a neurological difference that made it easier for Josie to relate to things such as machines and computers. But, although it was easy understanding machines, Asperger's made it much harder for Josie to know what to say or how to behave when around people. For one thing, Josie really didn't seem to get those unwritten rules on how people are supposed to behave.

For example, if Josie saw someone that smelled bad, she'd say,

"You smell bad!"

As far as Josie was concerned, she was right. She just didn't understand that there was a rule: if people smell (or look bad), you don't say it to others. Another thing that made it hard is that although Josie was great communicating with her words, she didn't understand that people also communicated with other things like their body language, or facial expressions (like making funny faces) and their tone of voice (saying things sarcastically).

She desperately wanted to fit in with others, but she just didn't know how. So Iris developed a game using picture cards for them to play while Josie fixed the machines. When Josie reacted with wrong behaviour, Iris would hold up a card that showed her the correct way to behave. Josie loved this game and she gradually began to remember what to say and how to act with people.
As spring came to an end, Josie had gotten a whole lot better in figuring out how to communicate with people. Plus, she had fixed most of Iris's broken machinery.

S U M M E R

Spring had passed quickly and the Riverbank Animals had been very busy. Each day, they took off to observe the town people and give out the Iris Cards to people who they noticed doing good deeds for children with mental health challenges. They were people who took the time to notice that although a child acted differently, perhaps there was a reason for it and they wanted to learn how to help that child.

Rosie Raccoon went to Josie's school, and noticed that Josie's teacher taught the class a lesson on Autism Spectrum Disorder. Rosie also appreciated the fact that the teacher didn't mention that Josie was one of the students with an ASD. Josie noticed that in the next few days the children seemed kinder to her and didn't criticize her as much.

Ottie Otter saw one of the coaches at the swimming pool giving extra help to a child who had Attention-Deficit Hyperactivity Disorder (ADHD). He found a way to help the child focus on his strokes and swim faster. He told the child he might one day be a great swimmer like Mike Brown and go to the Olympics.

Petunia Skunk was thrilled to see a group of people playing a game of basketball and including some children who had mental health challenges. She was afraid to put the Iris Cards in their pockets as they might see her and run away, so she left the cards in their knapsacks beside the court.

Dora Duck read an article in the town newspaper by the editor on the topic of supporting children with mental health challenges and how necessary it was to change the way people thought about these special needs children. So she waddled off to his office to leave an Iris Card.

Iris overheard one of the major business owners of the town speaking to his employees and telling them that the company would be hiring some children with mental health challenges for after school jobs and that he would be offering workshops at the store on how to assist these children in understanding how to do the job to the best of their ability.

Soon the whole town was talking about the Iris Cards. Where had these cards come from? Who was Iris? The townspeople decided to have a meeting to discuss this mystery.

They met at the town hall and many people attended including the parents of the children with mental health challenges. The mayor chaired the meeting and began by asking who had received the Iris Cards and what deed they had done. As the people spoke, they realized that they all had done something to recognize or help these children in a positive way.

They all decided that they wanted to do something really special for these children. One of the townspeople suggested a Walk. They could hold the Walk in the fall and have a route around the town. They decided to call it the **BRAVE NEW MINDS WALK.**

They would ask the local Children's Mental Health Agencies, schools and other community and parent organizations to help them organize the event. Many offered to sponsor a child or participate themselves. They had many wonderful ideas and were getting very excited about this project. They asked the parents if this might work and they agreed, but that the atmosphere had to be relaxing and not too noisy. The parents suggested the use of moon bounces and other sensory stations for the children to use at various places along the walk. The townspeople felt they could create such an atmosphere and set up many committees to organize the event.

Freddy Fox had been listening at the window and ran back to tell Iris and the Riverbank community.

Iris was so excited. She said,

"People like to help and make others feel good about themselves.

These children have been excluded from many activities in the town because people did not know how to treat them. But as the townspeople begin to understand how these children are affected by their conditions, they are realizing that these children have many special qualities."

One day, after Josie and Iris, had finished repairing another of Iris's contraptions, Josie said to Iris.

"People are being kinder to me now and seem to like me better.

They don't stare at me and say mean things anymore."

"Your town is becoming a more caring community,"

said Iris.

"We all need to be treated with respect and courtesy. It actually makes everyone feel better when we are nice to each other."

All seemed to be going as Iris had hoped except for the Bullies, as they still liked to tease Josie whenever they could until something drastic happened that changed their behaviour forever.

One day Josie was working on her bike on her front porch when the Bully Boys rode by. They decided to tease Josie and got off their bikes and walked up to her porch.

"Hey Josie, we really like your bike. I am going to take it for a spin,"

said one of the boys.

Josie was really scared that they would take her bike and she started to scream and yell at them and burst into tears when they grabbed her bike. Just then a neighbour of Josie's appeared from next door. She had received an Iris Card the other day as she had taken the time to ask Josie's mom what Asperger's Syndrome was and how she could help Josie.

She told the boys to stop teasing Josie and that she would notify their parents of their behaviour. The boys started to take off but just then a car came by and as they had left their bikes too near the road, the car drove over their bikes.

"Our bikes," screamed the boys.

"They are ruined."

"I can fix them for you," said Josie.

"I am really good at fixing bikes."

"You know how to fix these mountain bikes?"

exclaimed the boys.

"Sure, I can fix any bike.
Leave the bikes here and
I will fix them for you,"
stated Josie.

“That is so cool. You are really neat,”

declared the boys.

“We will be back tomorrow to help you fix our bikes and you can tell us what to do.”

After they left, Josie thanked her neighbour and said, “They want to be my friends.”

“Well, they have learned a good lesson. They did not know you at all and only noticed that you act different so they called you names and were mean to you. But when you said you would fix their bikes, they realized what a smart person you are and they felt badly that they had teased you. I am going to sit here with you for awhile to make sure you are OK,” said the neighbour. “And just to be on the safe side though, let’s make sure your mother will be around so they really do treat you nicely tomorrow.”

F A L L

Autumn arrived with all its beautiful colours. There was a softness in the air and the Riverbank Animals were busy stocking their pantries for the long winter ahead. But everyone was very excited about the **BRAVE NEW MINDS WALK** which was in a few weeks.

The townspeople had all come together to put on this special occasion. Many had helped to get lots of people to sign up for the Walk. Others had organized the refreshments. One of the companies in town bought tee-shirts for all the walkers. The children felt important and were looking forward to the Walk. A few days before the event, Josie came to visit Iris at the Riverbank. Iris was in her garden picking her vegetables.

"Hi Iris," said Josie. "My parents and I can hardly wait for the Walk. A lot of our friends and family are going to participate and we all are getting neat tee-shirts. Iris, will you come to the **BRAVE NEW MINDS WALK**, too?"

"I would not miss it. All the Riverbank Animals will be there, although you may not see us. We are very proud of the way the town has responded to our **Iris Cards** and come together to be good citizens for children such as yourself. And we have a little surprise for you, too, Josie. When we first met, you said you would like to come to one of our tea parties. Well, we have decided to ask you to our annual Riverbank Christmas Tea Party as our guest of honour to celebrate all that you have done to help make your community a nicer place to live and recognize children with mental health challenges."

"That is so amazing.
I can't believe that I am going to come to one of your famous Riverbank Tea Parties," said Josie.

The day of the Walk arrived. It was a beautiful warm sunny day. Everyone had worked hard to make it a success. The mayor arranged that the walkers would march into the arena with the Town Band playing a relaxing tune. After the opening ceremonies, the participants started their walk around the town. Many carried banners that said things such as **"Walking to Raise Awareness for Children's Mental Health," "It's not Autism, its AWEtism," "Open Minds - Open Doors"** and **"Together We Can Make a Difference."** After the Walk, everyone gathered at the Park and every child received a medal. They set up more sensory stations and the children seemed quite relaxed and happy.

Everyone agreed that this day had been a great success and most of all; it brought the whole town together in understanding and including these special children into the community. They decided to make this an annual event.

AVE NEW
INDS WA

WINTER

Winter came early to the Riverbank Community, but the Riverbank Animals were all snuggled up in their homes. They enjoyed winter as it gave them a chance to visit and socialize with their neighbours. Of course the big event of the season was **The Riverbank Christmas Tea Party** at Iris's cave. It was held every year for all the Riverbank Community to come and celebrate the good things that had happened. This year they were honouring Josie and the introduction of the Iris Card Campaign. Josie arrived with her friends Skippy, Fish and Teeman and as they sat around enjoying the delicious feast, Iris asked everyone what they thought of the Iris Card Campaign.

Ottie was the first to speak. "I thought it was great fun and the townspeople really responded well to the cards."

Madeleine said, "I am amazed at how much friendlier the town has become and everyone seems much happier."

"Well, I noticed that there were no more bullies in the town," said Freddy Fox.

"It is not fun to be a bully."

"And I noticed that there seems to be less stigma toward children who have mental health challenges. People don't have the false ideas about these children that they had before," said Rosie Raccoon.

"Well it looks like we did what we hoped to do. We made the town a nicer place to live for everyone, especially Josie and all my special children," said Iris.

"I think we should keep up our Iris Card Campaign next year and I am also going to mention it on my website and put the Iris Cards on it for people to download and maybe other communities will start the Iris Card Campaign, too. You have all done a wonderful job of helping children with mental health disorders."

Josie sprang up and exclaimed to Iris and the Riverbank Animals:

"You can fix things too!"

Iris the Dragon Anti-Stigma Card Template

Iris has put her Card on this page for you to scan and use for your own Anti-Stigma Campaign in your community. Iris would be thrilled for you to use her Card and also organize a Brave New Minds Walks. Good luck and thank you for supporting children's mental health.

Epilogue

Epilogue by Dr. Mark Kaluzienski

Josie has Asperger's Disorder, one of the Autism Spectrum Disorders (ASDs), also known as Pervasive Developmental Disorders (PDDs). ASDs include Autistic Disorder (Autism), Asperger's Disorder, and Pervasive Developmental Disorder Not Otherwise Specified. They also include the less common Rett's Disorder and Childhood Disintegrative Disorder. ASDs are diagnosed when children's development of communication and social skills does not follow the expected course. Children with ASDs are often inflexible and prefer predictability and sameness. They tend to think, talk and understand the world in a literal, concrete manner. In addition, they often have some problems with motor skills, can have peculiar sensory sensitivities, and may engage in unusual repetitive behaviours or have an area of intense special interest.

Asperger's Syndrome is diagnosed when a variety of Autism-like behaviours are present, but not to the extent or degree that can be associated with Autism. In Asperger's Disorder, language, cognition and self-help skills develop as expected. However despite appropriate speech and language skills, communication is still difficult and often done in unusual ways. As a developmental disorder Asperger's is present from birth but may not be noticeable until about two years of age when language and socializing becomes more complex and important. Like Josie, kids with Asperger's tend to be "loners". Josie is very good at rules for games, but she has a hard time with rules for being polite. Talking and playing with others is difficult as social rules don't come naturally and she doesn't understand body language or facial expressions. It is hard for her to interpret and appropriately react to what might be on the mind of someone simply by seeing them or hearing them talk. Josie talks in an unusual way and usually it's about her small number of passionate interests such as bicycles. She is direct and concrete so she uses the literal meanings of words and just blurts out what she is thinking. For most people interacting with others comes quite naturally, but for Josie and others with Asperger's it takes a great deal of work. By looking at Josie's story we can learn what life is like for Josie and how to help her feel good and get along with others.

Just as Josie has a hard time understanding how she can hurt other people's feelings, she also has a hard time understanding her own feelings. Occasionally, using certain learning strategies can help ease these difficulties, but only partially. Iris used cards to show Josie proper behaviour. Cards with pictures of people can demonstrate what different kinds of emotions look like. Then Josie was taught how to express each emotion in ways that don't get people upset. She then started to identify the same emotions and behaviours in other people and learned how to respond to them and talk about them in public. Once Josie saw that she experiences the same emotions as everyone else, she didn't feel so different anymore. This helped her appreciate that other people get hurt the same way she does and to be more empathic and patient. Using social stories where the story characters explain what they are feeling and why can provide specific examples for children with Asperger's. Memorizing common questions and answers will make responding to situations easy and automatic even before they are fully understood. Removing the fear and uncertainty around talking with others will make it less stressful and more pleasant to be around other people. This may be important as attempts are made to draw them away from their areas of special interest. Josie learned that people can be just as fun as bikes once she learned how to socially interact with them.

How else could Iris have helped Josie? More tea parties! Josie's Asperger's makes it much harder for her to learn how to talk and play with others. Unfortunately, much of Josie's experience with other children is getting ridiculed and bullied. Over time she may feel that being a bully is the normal way to act! Having a tea party with the polite river animals might demonstrate for Josie how to talk and act with others. Since we all don't live near Iris' riverbank, some children with Asperger's can learn a lot from social skills groups that provide direct instruction in social communication and social norms. Many organizations provide these types of programs. Parents can also have fun participating in imaginary play, taking on fun roles and acting out scenes where some social rules also come into play. Even regular games and sports teach sharing, turn taking, and patience. Of course this will be challenging for kids with Asperger's, so start small but be persistent. Remember that what seems obvious to us is lots of work for children like Josie. So use lots of reminders and repetition, and congratulate them on their hard work. Whenever possible make it fun! Nobody wants to work all day long.

Children with Asperger's tend to have certain routines and have a hard time adjusting to changes. Rules can be rigidly followed and very literally interpreted. Iris would always tell Josie in advance what they would be doing the next day. This prepared Josie for new activities and learning. Having a written schedule with a warning before the activity is about to change is helpful to some children with Asperger's. Also remember that being strict with rules can also be a helpful quality of children with Asperger's. Learning how to play with other children can be scripted as a new routine with new rules to follow. By preparing ahead, being very clear, and moving slowly much progress is possible. Pay attention to how each child learns. Some children with Asperger's are very visual, and respond best to pictures and visual plans. For them 'talking things through' could be very stressful. If they are upset show them a card with their favourite way of calming down. Take out your camera or markers and let your creative side have some fun while you set up an environment for a child with Asperger's to thrive. Other children remember best what is heard. In this case repeating verbally is most helpful. Just remember to be specific and clear. Avoid abstract jargon and be concrete and definitive. Telling a child with Asperger's they need to 'Pull up their socks' could be very confusing. Instead tell them clearly 'I need you to sweep the floor everyday at 4pm.' For all children with ASDs, Social Stories can be written to describe a specific situation, a new routine or skill, or abstract concept using the guidelines such as those developed by Carol Gray (1998). Topics are identified by the individual child's unique experiences and social responses and provide the child with important information about social events using positive language.

Josie is talented in remembering details and rules, but has problems with talking with other kids. You can imagine why she enjoys bikes more than making friends. Many kids with Asperger's feel much more comfortable with computers, machines, or learning science. These "things" are predictable, don't have feelings to hurt, and never say mean things or bully. Iris added a new routine in helping Josie learn how to socialize with others by combining it with her old routine, fixing things. Josie felt comfortable with Iris because she allowed her time to fix her broken machines. By putting a limit on special interests, children with Asperger's can have regular periods of comfort between all the new learning they have to do. Josie also found out her love of bikes could help her make friends, not just make her different. By fixing the bullies' bikes she showed how she could make a meaningful contribution to other children. Josie could be a leader in teaching other kids how to fix things themselves, gaining confidence and learning even more social skills herself. Now that her interest in bikes is a social success, she may be more interested in learning about other things she can fix or help others with.

There are also things that we must do to accommodate children with Asperger's, not just demand that they change all on their own! Like many children with Asperger's Josie does not like loud noises such as at school rallies. Rough fabrics and loud noises can be overwhelming, reducing attention span and increasing anxiety. On the other hand some kids can stare at a flashing light or enjoy being squished under heavy blankets for hours. Determining what children find calming and what upsets them can be important. Taking a break in a quiet room may improve attention for kids sensitive to bright noisy classrooms. Squeezing a stress ball from time to time might be helpful to calm down. Or being able to run and do jumping jacks for a short period might help wake someone up. Josie loves to fix things and by breaking up learning with fixing Iris was able to help Josie out. Allowing time for special interests, accommodations for sensory sensitivities, and calming sensory breaks is essential. No one wants to work hard to fit into a world that they find uncomfortable all the time.

Put yourself in Josie's shoes. No one wants to hear all her encyclopaedic knowledge of bikes, she is bullied and teased, she hurts people's feelings and doesn't know why, and even helpful Iris says she needs to do extra work practicing getting along with people. You can imagine how much extra work Josie has to do everyday just to get through it, never mind succeed in getting along with others. It can be exhausting and overwhelming. This is when children and adolescents with Asperger's can have problems with anger, anxiety, and depression. Often this is demonstrated with aggression to others or other troubling behaviours. As much as these behaviours are distressing to see, they indicate a need that can't be expressed or a demand that exceeds their current ability or coping skills. Determining the source of the behaviour identifies how best to help a child work through it. This may involve changing the environment (e.g. taking a test in a quiet resource room), reducing the demand (e.g. talking at desk instead of in front of the class), or skills training (e.g. how to talk in front of a group).

Josie is a great example of a child with Asperger's Disorder. Her experiences give us insight into what it's like to have Asperger's and how to try and work with it, instead of against it. With Asperger's there is difficulty communicating, especially using non-verbal communication, and learning social rules. Relating to other children and being empathic does not come naturally. Understanding machines and technology is easier as it builds upon their strengths for following rules and concrete literal thinking. There are often sensory sensitivities that can contribute to problems with attention, anxiety, and behaviour. Despite these similarities each child with Asperger's is unique in the number and intensity of these traits. They are also individual in how they cope and respond to their challenges. Just as you have learned from Josie's story, we best learn about a child with Asperger's from their personal story. By entering their world we can meet them where they are, and working from their perspective, move slowly to a place of mutual understanding.

To begin this understanding let us consider learning hockey. Many children desire to be hockey stars yet we are not born knowing how to play hockey. First they must learn balance and coordination. Learn to stand, start, and stop moving with skates on slippery ice. Then comes grasping and controlling the stick. Followed by figuring out how to move and shoot the puck...and ultimately putting it all together with teamwork to make the play! Each step builds upon the last. We do not jump to playing the game without practice or knowledge of the rules. Each child is assessed for their skill level and put into the appropriate training level. For children with Asperger's interacting and socializing with others is like learning hockey. They are not born with the skills or knowledge of the rules. Yet, because it is natural for most people to have those skills, they often expect children with Asperger's to be "hockey stars". So we need to assess their areas of strength and weakness, and work from there.

If you suspect that someone you know may have Asperger's Disorder or another Pervasive Developmental Disorder it is important to get a thorough assessment by a professional familiar with the diagnosis. Child psychiatrists, psychologists, developmental paediatricians, or neurologists most commonly diagnose this condition. A detailed developmental history is important. This includes milestones such as first words, first sentences, type of play preferences, and how toys were used. Once a diagnosis of ASD is made it is important to learn as much about it as you can and come up with a plan of action. Many professionals can help with this depending on the needs of each child. Occupational therapists can help with special sensory needs or learning strategies. Speech and language pathologists can help with speech and social communication difficulties. Behavioural consultants can help find the root cause of behavioural problems and suggest modifications for home and school. Finally psychologists can provide strategies for coping with anxiety and anger such as Cognitive Behavioural Therapy. They also do assessments to make sure an appropriate school placement is made, and suggest learning strategies for the classroom. Just as Josie had Iris and the riverbank animals, each child with ASD needs their own support team to help them along.

Suggested Reading

- Complete Guide to Asperger's Syndrome, by Tony Atwood, 2006.
- More Than a Mom: Living a Full and Balanced Life When Your Child Has Special Needs, by Amy Baskin and Heather Fawcett, 2006.
- The OASIS Guide to Asperger Syndrome: Completely Revised and Updated, by Patricia Romanowski Bashe, 2005.
- Look Me in the Eye: My Life with Asperger's, by John Robison, 2008. An incredible book that describes what it is like to have Asperger's by someone who has it.
- Gray, Carol. (1998). Social Stories and comic strip conversations. In Schopler, E., Mesibov, G., & Kunce, L. (Eds.), Asperger Syndrome or High-Functioning Autism? New York: Plenum Press.

Useful Websites

- Autism Society of Canada: www.autismsocietycanada.ca
- Autism Society of America: www.autism-society.org
- American Academy of Child and Adolescent Psychiatry: www.aacap.org
- Autism Ontario has a detailed list of educational resources: www.autismontario.com
- Online Asperger Syndrome Information and Support: www.aspergersyndrome.org
- "Understanding the Student with Asperger Syndrome: Guidelines for Teachers" by Karen Williams, 1995, FOCUS ON AUTISTIC BEHAVIOR, Vol. 10, No. 2. www.udel.edu/bkirby/asperger/karen_williams_guidelines.html